CONTE

1. Just Like Vinyl	1
2. The Hottest Day	4
3. Worry, Worry, Worry	7
4. Make It Count	11
5. The Next Act At The Divine Comedy	14
6. First Draft	17
7. Why They Chew Us	20
8. Extraction	23
9. Clean Energy	26
10. The Nothing At The Edge Of The Universe	30
Afterword	35

I

JUST LIKE VINYL

THRUM
"...Scratch."
"What...where are we?" said Wilkins. His voice was thick with confusion.

"We've been here before," said the professor.

Wilkins looked at the volcano erupting in the distance, and ducked to avoid a swooping pterodactyl.

"Are you sure? I would have thought I would remember."

"I don't remember either," said the professor. "But my calculations predicted the possibility, and I'm sure..."

THRUM

"...that's what's happened."

"You mean something's gone wrong?" said Wilkins, trying not to fall out of the tree they were now in. This seemed important, given the sabre toothed tiger below.

"The device failed! We are..."

THRUM

"...trapped. We are skipping through time, again and again. Maybe forever."

Wilkins looked sadly out over the vast, broken landscape. Now it held only rubble and bones.

"How?"

"We must have ripped the fabric of time," said the professor. "Like on an old fashioned vinyl. You know. Like a..."

THRUM

The End

TEN TINY STORIES

2
THE HOTTEST DAY

"That's right, the hottest on record," said Flint, fetching his customer a bag of ice. "Twice as hot as last summer! Better stock up!"

It was true: the little reality bubble had got stuck between a story about a desert planet and one set in the heart of a star. Narrative resonances were leaking. The reality bubble was heating up fast.

Everyone was scared. Where would it all end?

Everyone was scared, that is, except Flint.

"Don't you want to be saving some of that ice for yourself?" asked his customer.

"Why bother?" said Flint. "I've seen this sort of thing a million times. Lot of drama about nothing. It's bound to sort itself out. They always do."

"Maybe we should move the bubble out of the way of those blistering stories we're trapped between?" asked another customer.

"Tush!" said Flint. "That'd be bad for business! Have you got any idea how much ice I'm selling those guys? Nah, I think we should stay put. I'm making a fortune!"

Just then, Flint's shop caught fire.

"Not to worry," said Flint, opening the trap door, "down we all go. We'll be quite safe down here while the fires sort themselves out."

Flint led them down to a tiny apartment he kept in the core of the reality bubble. There were no flames here, but it was still hot.

"Maybe now is the time to, ah, get away from those hot stories?" suggested one of the customers timidly.

"Nonsense!" said Flint. "Very good for your average ecosystem, a conflagration. It'll sort everything out. Just you wait."

They waited. It got hotter and hotter. Suddenly, one of Flint's customers caught fire.

"Argh!" said the customer.

"Some people," said Flint, shaking his head sadly, "will complain about anything. Stop panicking. It will all be fine. You'll see."

There was a loud *whuffing* noise, as the last of the little reality bubble went up in a puff of superheated narrative particles.

Everything was very silent.

Flint had been right, after all. The fires had completely gone out.

The End

JAMIE BRINDLE

3
WORRY, WORRY, WORRY

"But there's something wrong," said Terri, wringing her continents anxiously. "I know there is. I can just feel it in my plates."

The doctor leant back and shook his head.

"You're mistaken," he told her. "You're the healthiest planet I've ever met. You're imagining things. You must try not to work yourself up."

Terri nodded miserably. It was true: she had always been a worrier. Even when she was no more than a cooling globule of magma, she had been convinced she would set in the wrong shape.

"Well, if you say so, doctor," she sniffled. "I'll try to forget about it."

But that night, Terri couldn't get to sleep. A terrible itching troubled her. As soon as she scratched one of her river deltas, the itching sprung up on a tundra. She rubbed at her tundra, and then the itching was one her rich rainforests, tingling and aching as if it were on fire.

But the next day, the doctor was still unimpressed.

"I can't see a thing!" he told her, after examining her surfaces most carefully. "Really, Terri, you must try to get a grip. You're such a hypochondriac. In reality, you're perfectly healthy. If you're not careful, you'll work yourself up so much you'll flip your magnetic field!"

"But...but isn't there anything you can do?" she begged.

"I can take some surface scrapings, see if there is anything to be grown," the doctor told her. "I am quite certain, however, that they will come back negative."

"What will I do then?" asked Terri, feeling desperate.

The doctor shrugged.

"It's all psychological," he told her. "You need to spend some time in one of the new institutes. I know a wonderful black hole in Andromeda. A few millennia in there, I'm sure you'll be quite a different planet."

That sounded ominous.

"I'd really rather wait until the scrapings are back," she told him.

The doctor looked bored.

"Suit yourself," he said.

For a while after that, the itching seemed to go away.

"Maybe the doctor was right," Terri said to herself. "Perhaps it is all in my head, after all."

But that night, the symptoms started up again. This time, they were worse than ever. The itching was everywhere now. No amount of scratching helped.

Her head was spinning. Her whole atmosphere seemed packed with a vile smoke. And she was so hot! She didn't sleep a wink that night; in the morning, she made her way back to the surgery.

"Guess what?" the doctor greeted her. He looked rather pleased with himself.

"What?" asked Terri.

"The surface scrapings came back positive! You were right all along!"

A wave of fear flushed through her. She knew it! She just knew it! She was sick! She had something terrible!

"Am I...going to die?" she managed to gasp out.

But the doctor gave a laugh.

"Die? Of course not!" he said. "Oh, no, what you've got is quite rare and rather uncomfortable, but certainly nothing to worry about."

"What is it?"

"An infestation," he told her. "Nasty little buggers. Once they get a hold, they play havoc with your ecosystems."

"That doesn't sound like nothing," said Terri uncertainly.

The doctor came closer, and began examining her features carefully.

"Textbook," he said in an abstracted voice. "Melting icecaps, sea level rising, pollutants in your atmosphere. Oh yes. I could write a paper on you, that's for sure!"

"My icecaps are melting!" gasped Terri. "But surely that's awful! Please, please, please: what is the treatment?"

"Oh don't worry, you silly planet," the doctor told her affectionately. "The symptoms are nasty for a few thousand years, but we don't need to treat it."

Terri started to ask why, but already she was feeling better. Her seas were rising, washing the awful itch from her surface. Her atmosphere was poisoned, but it was the infestation itself that was being poisoned by it.

"I think I'm going to be alright," she said.

"Yes," agreed the doctor happily. "That's the thing about humans. They're tenacious little critters, but they are a self-limiting illness."

The End

JAMIE BRINDLE

❦ 4 ❧
MAKE IT COUNT

"Vote out!" said Thistle, waving his placard and jutting out his lip.

Around him, the hurly-burly flow of entities eddied and swirled. There were so many types. Gods and sprites, mist-gobblers and sun-squibs, poor souls from the Beginning and ghosts from the very end. That was the problem, Thistle thought. It had become far too confusing. Too much diversity. After all, there wasn't room for everyone.

In the afternoon came the vote. To Thistle's great delight, an "Out" result was reached. That evening, they began to pour away. They leached off, slipping out of the dimming bubble of reality, taking with them their songs and their shimmerings, leaving the place still and cold.

"But so much more ordered!" thought Thistle. "So much cleaner!"

For a week, he was happy. Then a feeling of disquiet began to grow. There was still a problem, after all.

"Vote out!" said Thistle again. This time, his placard showed a devastating breakdown of all the damage the other dimensions were doing to their little reality bubble.

"It's true!" he said, when questioned. "What has Depth ever done for us? And don't even get me started on Time..."

The big day came, and sure enough Thistle got his way. Things were much more suitable, so much more simple now there was only Length to worry about.

Thistle was happy for a long time, then - or he would have been, if there had been any Time left in the reality bubble to be happy within - but then he began once more to grow restless.

"Vote Out!" he said. "This nonsense has got to stop! Out, out, out!"

And when the vote came, Thistle was vindicated, cast out of the last dregs of the reality bubble by a majority of one to zero. He had been the last sensical thing left at that point, and it was clearly time for him to go. The tiny bubble was much tidier without him; and he was much happier without a self to loathe, which was, of course, the whole problem in the first place.

The End

TEN TINY STORIES

5
THE NEXT ACT AT THE DIVINE COMEDY

God was sweating, so nervous he could hardly stand.

"Tough crowd tonight," whispered Anubis.

The place was teeming. In one corner, Thor and Loki were practicing their slapstick double-act. By the bar, Allah had an audience of Chinese deities and was telling knock-knock jokes. On stage, Zeus was finishing up.

"Anyway folks, you've been wonderful," he said, flashing his trademark smile and forking lightning upwards. "Now please give it up for a very good friend of mine. Everyone's favourite monotheistic deity - well, one of the top two, anyway - God!"

There was deafening applause, and Zeus strutted offstage.

"You're up," hissed Anubis. "Don't worry, you're gonna kill! Just keep it light!"

God shuffled onstage. Everything went very quiet. Even Thor had stopped tying Loki's neck into a knot, and was regarding him coolly.

"Uh, hello," said God.

Just imagine them naked, he thought. This didn't help, because many of them were naked already, particularly those who specialised in love or lust or both.

Why did this always happen? No matter how hard he prepared, no matter the quality of his material, he always died on stage.

"So, uh, I was talking to my therapist..." God began.

"Speak up!" someone yelled, to general amusement.

God stuttered to a halt.

He was frozen. Nothing would come. None of the witty stories, none of the satirical gems.

What could he do? He was dying out here!

Then he had an idea.

Moving quickly, he cobbled together a few makeshift dimensions. He plucked a void into existence, made sure there was no form or substance, then sighed.

If the crowd wanted something lowbrow, he would give it to them.

"Let there be light," he said ironically.

With a bang, the little Universe got going.

After that, the laughter was pretty much constant.

The End

❦ 6 ❦
FIRST DRAFT

She was born, of course, then had a childhood. At fifteen she was pretty but unwise; thus her dreams of university melted in dirty nappies.

By twenty three she was studying and her life was back on track - or rather, had she ever left it? For she loved her son, fiercely and more than she had ever herself been loved by anyone.

At thirty seven, she remarried; and in the same year, her son died a stupid, pointless death. The marriage spluttered all summer, then failed.

It looked at as if she would fail, too: whisky bottles, bankruptcy, a minor criminal record. But the suicide attempt was botched, and she found music in her fiftieth year - an unlikely saviour - and spent the last of her middle age sober in pubs and clubs singing all the old songs in new ways.

She was happy, for a while. Then came the pain, and after two months, the diagnosis. An operation nearly saved her; nearly, but not quite.

"So," said god, "what do you think?"

"What do you mean?" she asked him, looking around and wondering where her body was.

"Oh, I know it's a bit rough yet," god continued, "but I must say, I'm rather proud of it. Your life. Good for a first draft, I mean. Needs some of the details ironing out, of course. What did you make of it?"

She thought for a moment.

"Did there have to be so much pain?" she asked.

"Oh, absolutely," said god. "No good having Christmas every day, so to speak."

She shrugged.

"Pretty good then," she said. She thought a bit more. "I liked the blues," she added.

"My point exactly," said god, happy she understood.

There was a silence.

"What happens now?" she asked.

"I suppose we better get those details ironed out," said god. "Now then, what should we change?"

She smiled, and they talked.

There was a flash of light.

She was born, of course.

The End

7
WHY THEY CHEW US

Klexo, Devourer Of Souls, paused amidst her endless feasting.

"But...but why?" she asked.

"It's more painful," answered The Chains, who was the one to tell of the edict.

"We've never had to before," protested Fex of the Bloody Tooth.

"Orders is orders," said Chains. "And you thought the new boss was soft."

"He is soft," said Klexo. "What else would you call letting them back out? Even after a thousand years."

"Reincarnation," said Chains morosely.

The daemons paused. The sound of piteous screaming drifted through Hell.

"There must be another reason," said Klexo, crunching her latest victim. "Swallowed whole was good enough before."

There was a gentle pattering noise as the torn fragments of another soul were washed down into the shared stomachs of Hell.

"I know why," said Fex smugly. "Worked it out."

He tossed another pleading soul into his mouth and chewed, as per the new edict.

"Well?" demanded the others.

"Cross pollination, innit?" said Fex. "As long as he's sending them back out, makes sense. Mix them up. We get the worst down here."

A happy enlightenment spread through Hell

"Well that's different," said Klexo. "I'm more than happy to chew for that!"

And the daemons chewed, happy in the knowledge that they were helping to blend the souls of murderers with rapists, thieves with matricides; and when the wheel turned once more, the evil that walked the earth would be all the sweeter.

The End

JAMIE BRINDLE

8

EXTRACTION

The throbbing in Tom's jaw was like a box of bees. He couldn't imagine a pain worse.
"But I saw the damn dentist last month!" he complained. "I ain't made of money."
He tried to hold out another day, but it just got worse.
"How much will you charge to take the tooth?" he demanded.
The dentist told him. It was too much.
Tom cursed.
"You could sell me the pain, instead," suggested the dentist.
Tom had heard about such things, but he was wary.
"You won't go taking nothing but the pain?" he asked. He had good memories he wanted to keep, strawberries in the sun with Lisa, and his mother's voice when he was a lad, and the feel of his son's hand in his own. Technology wasn't perfect. Mistakes had been made.
"Not a thing," promised the dentist. He strapped Tom in and put the induction helmet in place.
THRUM! Went the machine.
And, CLICK!
And, "Wow!" said Tom, sudden relief flooding his mouth. The

pain had vanished. Where it had been there was just a silky, blank whiteness in his mind.

"All done," said the dentist. "A clean extraction."

Tom nervously prodded his memories. Everything seemed in order. And after all, there was no pain.

The dentist paid Tom the agreed price for a grade III toothache. When Tom had left, the dentist logged via secure server to the Department of Corrections and uploaded the pain, for which he was paid twice as much as he had paid Tom.

"Ow!" shouted the convict the next day, when the toothache was applied. "Stop! Please, stop!"

"And you won't ever do it again?" said the Judge.

The convict swore he would not.

He left whistling. The first thing he did was buy a whole basket of strawberries.

The End

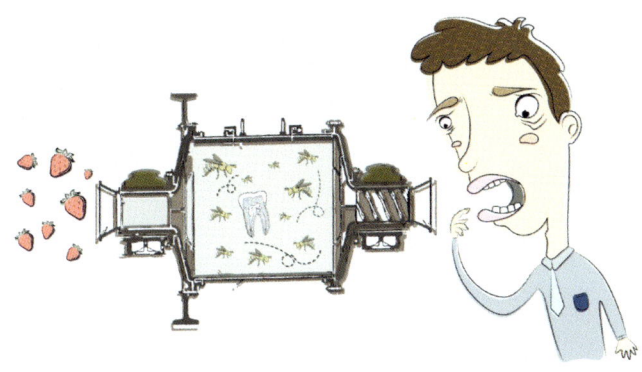

9

CLEAN ENERGY

"But it's so fast!" exclaimed the investor. "You can't tell me this thing runs on electricity?"

Bill danced his new car gracefully up through the gears. The wind roared in his ears, but there was no other noise. The engine, of course, was completely silent.

"It's not electric," he said, smiling smugly. "It's much better than that."

They overtook a police car. Bill didn't care. No other vehicle had a hope of catching them.

"What then?" gasped the investor. "Not...not nuclear?"

But Bill shook his head. Nuclear energy was a thing of the past. Or rather, with his new technology it soon would be.

"It runs," he said softly, "on immoral thoughts."

The investor laughed, but when Bill didn't join in, he looked thoughtful.

"I thought you were an environmentalist," complained the investor.

"I am," said Bill. "But expelling a bad thought into the ether is much better than expelling noxious fumes. Or radioactive waste."

The investor nodded. This sounded plausible.

That afternoon, Bill signed the contracts, and his new invention went into production.

Soon the roads were full of Bill's new cars. Sleek, silent vehicles zipping along clean roads. The air was pristine again. The ground and sea were no longer torn open in an increasingly savage quest for oil.

"Burglary," thought the drivers, as they slid along silent roads. "Theft and battery and fraud." A few bad thoughts seemed a reasonable price to pay.

But it wasn't long before the cars started slowing down.

"What's going on?" demanded the investor. "This is terrible! People will be wanting their money back!"

"Oh, it's just the narrowing of the potential difference," explained Bill, unlocking his car and waving in his bodyguard, before starting the engine with a brief image of an old lady being savaged by stoat. Things were much more dangerous nowadays. That was the problem with putting bad ideas into the air. The bad ideas were having the tendency to leech out into bad behaviours. Still, it was much more environmentally responsible than filling the air with carbon. Wasn't it?

"All people have to do is up their game," explained Bill, skilfully manoeuvring the car through a district of burning public buildings. "Just...just think big, you know?"

And that evening, after the investor ran the desperate ad campaign explaining how people could get their cars working again, everyone understood.

The cars whizzed once more. They were faster than ever.

"Rape," thought the drivers, urging their machines on to ever greater speeds. "Rape and slaughter and death."

But before long, the machines began to slow once more. This time, however, there was nothing more to be done.

"You are all just being prudish!" protested Bill, as the rioting crowd hauled him out of his sleek, beautiful car and marched him up the hill towards where the fires roared, huge and deadly. "It's just thoughts, after all! What's the harm of a few bad thoughts?

Look at the amazing engine I gave you!"

But the engine no longer ran, for the gradient had been equalised - the air was full of bad thoughts now, so thick and nasty you couldn't turn your head without knocking into one.

"This is wrong!" screamed Bill. "Burning people is wrong!"

But as they hurled Bill into the fires, there wasn't even one person left who knew if that was true.

The End

TEN TINY STORIES

10
THE NOTHING AT THE EDGE OF THE UNIVERSE

There was a scraping noise. It sounded like bones grinding on iron.

Dili frowned and turned the machine off. All was quiet. She unstrapped and got out of the cockpit.

Outside, the world was dark and the air was full of dust. She inspected the drill.

The head was blunted, smashed to smithereens.

Which was impossible. The drill had gone through everything so far, absolutely everything. It had taken her here, down, down, down, all the way from the surface and her old, useless life.

"Wotcher!" said a friendly voice. "Cor, that's a nice bit of kit!"

A being loomed out of the darkness. He was large and hairy. He had missing teeth and a friendly smile.

Dili scowled.

"It was," she said. "What the bloody hell's this? Why can't I get through?"

She gave the darkness that had blunted her drill a kick. It felt hard, harder than anything.

"Ow," added Dili.

"It's the Edge," explained the being.

"The edge of what?" asked Dili, suspiciously.

"Of everything," said the being. "The Universe."

Dili's frown deepened.

"I'm going through," she told him firmly. "You can't stop me."

"I don't need to stop you," said the being affably.

"I've come all this way," went on Dili, and it was true. She had started after she had lost her job, been kicked out of her flat, and her dog had been killed all in the same day. She had decided enough was enough. Reality really wasn't her thing any more.

"I can see that," said the being, peering back up the shaft Dili had drilled down. "Is that Asgard I see twinkling up there?"

"Yup," said Dili. She inspected the drill heads. They had been made of diamond reinforced with pure determination she had sublimated out of her own soul. They had gone through everything so far, but now they were worn completely flat.

"And that looks like Mount Olympus further off," went on the being. "And Hell beyond that. And..."

"I've been through a lot of places," snapped Dili. "None of them were right. I've had enough of all of them. I need to keep going."

And she kicked the darkness again to underline her position, but not quite so hard as before, because she didn't see the point of having a broken toe.

The being whistled.

"Looks like you're in a fix," he told her.

She glowered at him.

"Well, what the hell am I meant to do now?" she demanded.

The being shrugged.

"Go back?" he suggested.

"Out of the question," she told him flatly.

"Thought you'd say that," said the being. "But this is the Edge! You have to understand, there's nothing beyond. Nothing!"

And that was all it took; Dili had an idea.

She darted back into her machine and began rooting around.

"It's no good," said the being. His voice was calm, but if you had looked closely - very closely - you might have thought he seemed a little worried.

Where was it? Where was it?

Dili threw unwanted items out over her shoulder. A lightning bolt won from Thor fair and square in a game of chance. A clutch of swamp fairies she had rescued from the Deathlands, which she had picked up because she had felt sorry for them. And here...

...here it was.

Dili emerged, holding the thing she had been looking for. She had known it had been back there somewhere.

It was very light, of course. It weighed almost nothing.

"What - ah - what is that?" asked the being. He definitely sounded nervous now.

Dili held it up. It shimmered softly, a half light of diaphanous half-colours.

"A poor soul," she said. "From The Land Before Life. Completely lacking in experience. Not an iota of personality or weight. Utterly, utterly empty."

The being relaxed.

"Oh, one of them," he said, quite dismissive again. "Well I don't know what you think you'll achieve with that. It's not nearly as sharp or hard as your drill was, and that was blunted the moment it touched the Edge."

Dili smiled. It was a sharp smile. A smile with an edge of its own.

"Oh yes, I know that," she said, placing the Poor Soul softly against the nothing, and standing back. "I'm not going to try cutting through the nothing again. I know that's not possible."

There was a dreadful, dull creaking noise.

The being's eyes widened. Panic filled his face.

"What are you doing?" he demanded.

"You said yourself that nothing can cut through that Edge." Dili shrugged. "Doesn't mean the Edge can't cut through to here, though."

There was another creak, and a crack sprung into being. It ran the whole length of the Edge, from here to there and back again.

The Universe shuddered. The nothing was getting ready to break through.

"I've always thought it must be very lonely being the nothing at the Edge of the Universe," she whispered, almost talking to herself now. "More than anything it must want to find someone, anyone. Someone as empty as itself. I'm betting it would do anything to reach someone like that."

The being sprang forward, but it was too late.

The crack opened wide, the Edge slicing down the middle of the Universe. The nothingness beyond poured in, undoing, resolving, sweeping it all away.

Dili closed her eyes.

She had found her way out, at last.

When it took her, she was smiling.

The End

JAMIE BRINDLE

AFTERWORD

These ten tiny stories first appeared on my website and were emailed out to my subscribers, though they have mostly now been replaced by new stories. To make sure you don't miss any of these stories as they come out, make sure you are subscribed to my newsletter. You can sign up at my website, www.jamiebrindle.com - if you sign up, I'll also send you a free copy of my novella, *All Quiet In The Western Fold*!

AFTERWORD

THE ARTISTS

I am enormously happy to have been able to get such lovely art to illustrate these tiny stories. I am very grateful to all the artists.

Just Like Vinyl; The Hottest Day; Worry, Worry, Worry; First Draft; Clean Energy; The Nothing At The End Of The Universe - All these were illustrated by Olesya Hupalo. She is very talented - you can also find her work by following The Cup Of Arts on Instagram and Twitter, as well as Fiverr.

Make It Count - Silviana Stinghie, who you can find on Fiverr.

The Next Act At The Divine Comedy Store - agnes_digital on Fiverr.

Extraction - elio_leo on Fiverr.

Why They Chew Us - viper1325 on Fiverr.

∼

ABOUT THE AUTHOR

Jamie Brindle has been writing stories for almost as long as he can remember. Sometimes, he even publishes them.

He has done various jobs over the years, including boomerang salesman, tractor driver, hedge maze attendant, and - most recently - doctor.

He writes because it would be intolerable to keep these things bottled up inside his head. Imagine the mess.

You can find all his books on amazon - there are quite a few to explore now - or look him up at www.jamiebrindle.com

He lives with his beautiful badgery wife and his young son, Ben.